BOCH
CENTER

THIS BOOK IS
PRESENTED TO

GABRIELLA

FOR THEIR PARTICIPATION IN
THE BOCH CENTER'S
IN SCHOOL RESIDENCY PROGRAM

FALL 2022

# THE RARE, TiNY FLoWeR

Kitty O'Meara

Illustrated by Quim Torres

T tra.publishing

Once, in a forest,

a bird
  dropped
    a seed.

It wasn't a sapling,
it wasn't a weed,
but a rare, tiny flower
that found light
and grew.

To some it looked red,

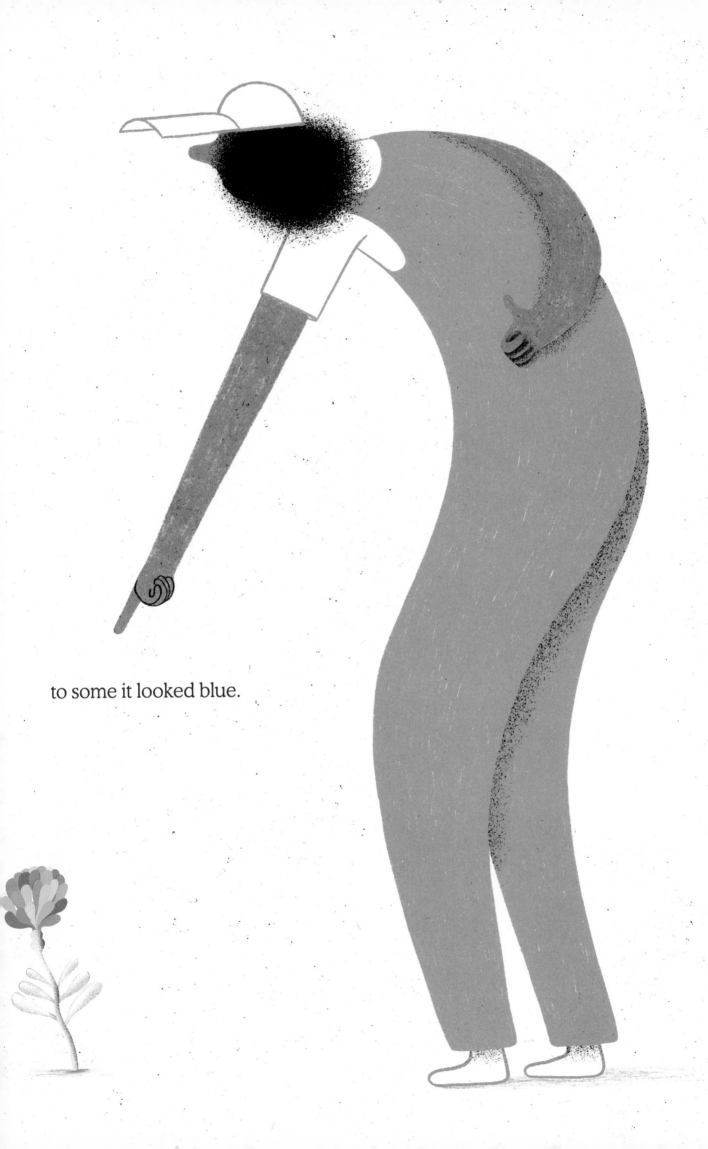

to some it looked blue.

Others saw yellow,
but many saw green.
A more puzzling flower
had never been seen!
A number saw umber,
a small group saw teal,

"We see it correctly! We see what is real!"

Each group insisted
its vision was right.
"Agree it's magenta,
or we'll
        start
            a fight!"

Powerful leaders
arrived, striking poses.
"We will not agree!"
And noses met noses.

Botanists came
to settle the score,
but couldn't decide,
so the leaders cried,

One pulled up the flower to shove in a vase,
as everyone hollered and argued their case.

The gifts of the flower risked being lost
as people drew lines that couldn't be crossed.

A little girl watched the loud confrontation,
then circled the flower in slow exploration.

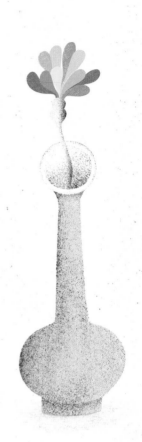

"Please, look again,"
came her calm, patient voice.
"Why?" cried the screamers.

She smiled. "There's a choice."

How could this be?
What could it mean?
What had she noticed
that they hadn't seen?

She lifted the vase,
and slowly rotated,
as all of the people
grew still, then elated...

For as the girl turned,
the colors changed places,
flashing a rainbow
across startled faces.

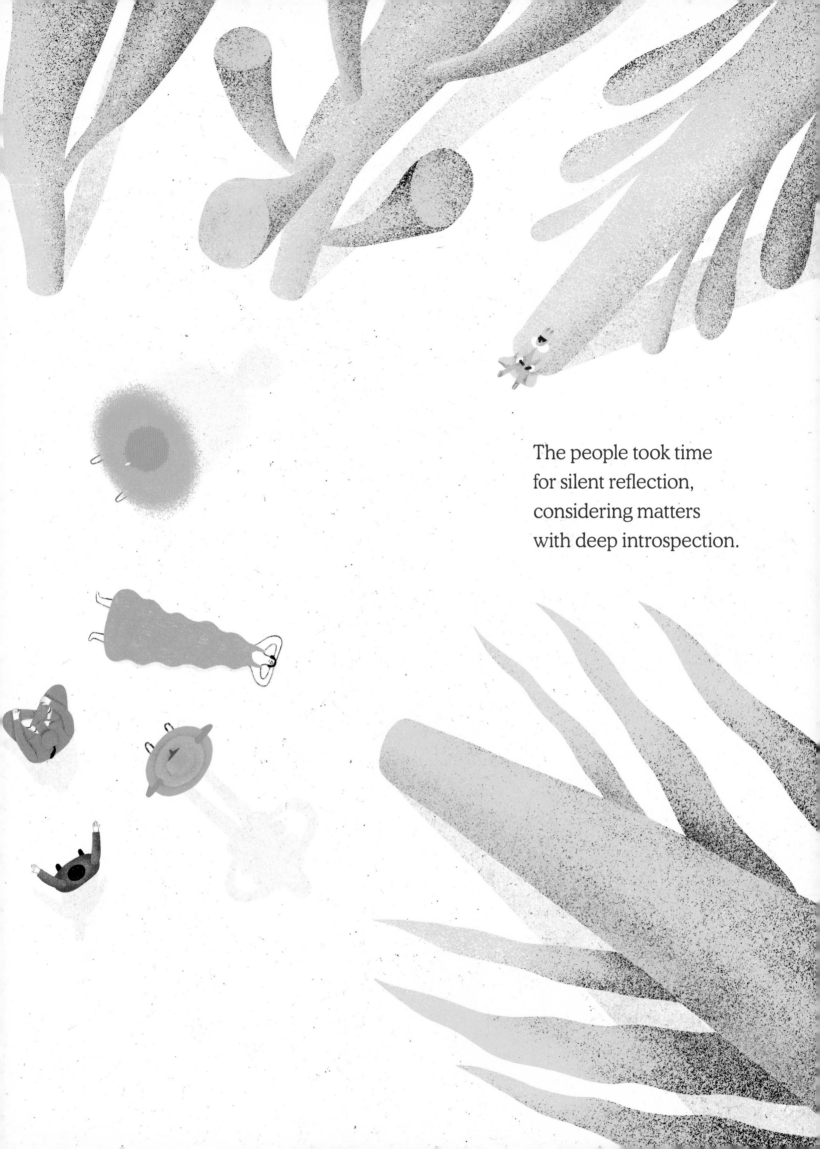

The people took time
for silent reflection,
considering matters
with deep introspection.

"Maybe there *are*
other colors to see;
what's lovely to you
*could* be lovely to me."

"What we now understand
to be utterly true
is how much depends
on *expanding* our view."

"It could be helpful
to breathe and be still,
*calmly* deciding
what won't work and will."

"Enjoying each color
and welcoming *all*,
creating a party
instead of a brawl."

"Oh, no!" the girl pointed,
"Look at the flower!
It's wilted and  faded,
and losing its power!"

Everyone watched
as the rainbow unspun.
What had their fighting
and selfishness done?

The rare, tiny flower
looked shriveled and weak.
Its petals were falling.
No one could speak.

The people were sad
and started to cry.
Had their ingratitude
caused it to die?

The girl very gently
returned it to earth.
Could it be nourished
and loved to rebirth?

Her tears showered down
and watered it
                ...then

the rare, tiny flower grew healthy again!

Its colors exploded, filling the sky, and everyone raised an exuberant cry!

All of the people, from all of the lands,
smiled and joyfully reached out their hands.
They danced and began composing a song
about being friendly and getting along.

When hearts come together, kindness can grow,
rainbows can happen more than we know!

So much to fix, too many false starts,
no time to waste in uniting our hearts.

All of creation is precious and rare,
and everyone has a color to share!

Life is for loving, and listening well,
and learning all colors have stories to tell!

The people were shining,
for they were new, too.
Each one considered
the other one's view.

A girl and a flower,
both small but courageous,
made loving all colors
quite wildly contagious.

The rare, tiny flower
shared wisdom that day...

A rainbow can happen when love leads the way.

# Talking with Author
# Kitty O'Meara

### What do you like best about writing?

I love that writing feels like magic. Things come out of you that you did not know were there. You have to sit and allow it to happen. When I wake up in the morning, I have no idea what twists my stories will take, and I love that.

### Is there anything about writing that you don't like?

Not really. Except that I don't have enough time to do as much of it as I want!

### Do your ideas for poems and stories always work out?

I don't develop some because I have so many ideas, and some interest me more than others. And sometimes story ideas fold into poems or other stories.

### Do you do other types of artwork in addition to writing?

I love to garden. Gardening is like painting but in three dimensions. You work with all kinds of textures and colors, and it takes attention and time, like writing a story in colors across the four seasons.

I also like to read, explore photography, and play with interior design. Both my husband and I enjoy making things. We make furniture and accent pieces, gifts for friends, and holiday decorations. We have a workshop and art room where we can design and create together.

### What other things do you like to do?

I get outdoors as much as I can. I like going for long walks. And my husband and I enjoy biking on the trail near our home. We live on a river and we can canoe together, and we like going out to shows and museums. And we love our four-leggeds. We have five rescue dogs and two cats.

**Where did the idea come from for *The Rare, Tiny Flower*?**
I think it was sparked when I noticed that people here and around the world were not listening to each other. Seriously, not listening. There was too much anger and fear from the pandemic and other sorrows that were crowding out our compassion. I was at home in lockdown and watching the news, feeling kind of sad about these things, and I had an image of this little flower planted in the middle of the woods, and a bird flying overhead that had dropped the seed.

**So the story began with an image.**
Yes, and that's what I mean by the magic of writing. Ideas and images float through our minds when we're considering things, and we have to pay attention and follow the journey of our ideas.

**How did the story then develop?**
The story evolved from there, connecting the tiny flower to the news that had saddened me. I think anger and fear may be useful ways to protect ourselves. But then we have to let them go and connect with each other, because that's the way problems are solved and how we add color to our lives. We have to notice all the little ways we're alike and all the little bits of the world that bless us every day. Something as insignificant as a rare, tiny flower can act as a reminder that we need to honor one another and one another's gifts, so we can share and care for the Earth and all living things together.

**What advice would you give to children who want to be creative—whether it is writing or visual art or music or dance or anything else?**
Do it! Play! Play with colors and paint and music and movement. Write stories and share them; write plays and act them out with your friends. Libraries are wonderlands, so visit them often. Some people think we need to spend a lot of money to be creative, but that's not true. Create!

**Is there anything you want to say to the children reading this book?**
I hope they enjoy it. I hope they have wonderful discussions about it with their parents, teachers, and friends. And I hope readers are reminded that there are always reasons to celebrate our humanity and the gift of life on Earth. Anger, fear, and hatred are no match, ever, for love.

For teachers everywhere, in gratitude for the magical and challenging
ways they lift up ideas and turn them for us to see every color
from every perspective. You are the rainbow-makers, widening
our capacity for wonder and connection.
—Kitty O'Meara

**The Rare, Tiny Flower**

Author
Text copyright © 2021 Kitty O'Meara

Illustrator
Illustrations copyright © 2021 Quim Torres

Publisher & Creative Director
Ilona Oppenheim

Art Director & Designer
Jefferson Quintana
ILONA Creative Studio

Editor
Andrea Gollin

Writing Credits
Interview with Kitty O'Meara: Andrea Gollin

Printing
Printed and bound in China by
Shenzhen Reliance Printers

Cover
Illustration: Quim Torres
Cover design: Jefferson Quintana

ISBN: 978-1-7347618-2-5
First Tra Publishing hardcover edition March 2022

*The Rare, Tiny Flower* is printed on Forest Stewardship Council certified paper
from well-managed forests.

Tra Publishing is committed to sustainability in its materials and practices.

Tra Publishing
245 NE 37th Street
Miami, FL 33137
trapublishing.com

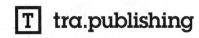